Pony-Crazed Princess

Princess Ellie's Starlight Adventure

Read all the adventures of Princess Ellie!

Pony-Crazed Princess

Princess Ellie's Starlight Adventure

by Diana Kimpton

Illustrated by Lizzie Finlay

Hyperion Paperbacks for Children
New York

For Rachel

First published in the United Kingdom in 2004 as
The Pony-Mad Princess: Princess Ellie's Starlight Adventure
by Usborne Publishing Ltd.
Based on an original concept by Anne Finnis
Text copyright © 2004 by Diana Kimpton and Anne Finnis
Illustrations copyright © 2004 by Lizzie Finlay

Printed in the United States of America
First U.S. edition, 2006
1 3 5 7 9 10 8 6 4 2

This book is set in 14.5-point Nadine Normal.
ISBN 0-7868-4873-1
Visit hyperionbooksforchildren.com

Chapter 1

"Princess Aurelia!" The shout echoed down the palace corridor.

Princess Ellie groaned. She was on her way to the stable and didn't want to stop. She didn't like to be called by her real name, either. She liked "Ellie" much more.

The owner of the voice came rushing toward the princess. It was a palace maid, who looked very flustered and out of breath.

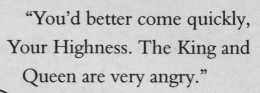

"You'd better come quickly, Your Highness. The King and Queen are very angry."

Ellie followed the maid back along the corridor, wondering what she'd done wrong this time. For once, she couldn't think of anything. She had been very polite for the last few days, and it had been a long time since she'd shown up for dinner in her jodhpurs or muddy boots.

The King and Queen were waiting impatiently for her in their favorite part of the royal garden. Their arms were crossed, and their faces looked even angrier than Ellie had expected.

"Look at the mess you've made, Aurelia," roared the King, as he pointed at the grass. The normally smooth green surface of the lawn was covered with hoofprints.

"How dare you ride in my garden?" wailed the Queen. She sniffed angrily and dabbed away a tear using a handkerchief embroidered with silver crowns. "It wasn't me," said Ellie.

"Don't tell lies," snapped the King.

Ellie resisted the temptation to snap back. She knew from experience that it would only make matters worse. "I am telling the truth," she insisted, as calmly as possible. "I've got all of the palace grounds to ride in. I don't need to use the royal garden."

"Hmmm," said the Queen thoughtfully. "Aurelia does have a point, my dear."

The King was less convinced. He stared suspiciously at Ellie and asked, "How do you explain the hoofprints, then?"

Ellie bent down and ran her fingers around one of the holes in the garden as she tried to think of an explanation. Meg, the royal groom, had a horse of her own, but she was too smart to ride Gypsy in the garden. Ellie's four ponies were the only other suspects.

"If you haven't ridden here, who has?" asked the Queen, when Ellie didn't answer. "It certainly wasn't Kate."

Ellie didn't need reminding. She had been lonely ever since her best friend had gone to visit her parents, who were working in a distant desert. Life was much more exciting and fun when Kate stayed with her grandmother, the palace cook. The two girls spent all their time together, riding Ellie's ponies or helping out at the stable. Once, they had even saved Sundance's life, after he somehow managed to get out of his stall in a storm.

That memory gave Ellie an idea. "One of the ponies must have escaped," she announced.

"That's a possibility," admitted the Queen. "But that doesn't mean we can have ponies running all over the place doing whatever they please."

"Definitely not," said the King, firmly. "Tell Meg to make sure it doesn't happen again."

Ellie promised that she would. Then she

ran to the stable to check on her ponies. To her surprise, none of them was missing. Moonbeam, Rainbow, Sundance, and Shadow were all in their stalls, happily munching hay. So was Gypsy.

"That's really strange," said Meg, when she heard what had happened.

"Maybe one of them escaped and then came back," suggested Ellie. "Sundance knows how to undo locks."

"He must have learned how to redo them, too," replied Meg. "His door was definitely closed tight this morning." She looked at Ellie's anxious face and smiled. "Don't worry. I'll double-check everything tonight before I go to bed, and I'll put a special clip on Sundance's door, so he can't undo it and get out."

"That should stop it from happening again," said Ellie, confidently. If there was no way her ponies could escape, there was no way they could do any damage. By the next morning, her parents would probably have forgotten all about the mysterious hoofprints.

Unfortunately, Ellie was wrong. Before she'd even had time for breakfast, she was summoned to the garden again, and so was Meg. Ellie's parents were even angrier than before. The King's face was nearly as red as the ruby in his crown.

"Look at this. There are even more hoof-prints than yesterday," said the King, as he stared accusingly at both of the girls.

"And my prize petunias are ruined," added the Queen, holding up the mangled plants.

"Your ponies have been eating my flowers."

"But they couldn't have been," said Ellie.

"They must have been," snapped the King.

"Excuse me, Your Majesties," said Meg, politely. "The ponies were all shut securely in their stalls when I went to bed last night, and they were still there this morning."

"Then they must have been out in between," said the Queen. "It's the only possible explanation. They are the only ponies at the palace."

The King glared at Meg. "This is your fault. Go back to the stable, and make sure this doesn't happen again. If it does, we may have to reconsider your position."

8

Ellie gasped with horror as Meg walked away. "You can't fire her, Dad. She hasn't done anything wrong."

"Are you admitting that you have, then?" asked her father, in a serious tone. "Were you lying about not riding here?"

"No," said Ellie. "But . . ."

"There are no buts about it," said the King, before she had time to finish. "It's Meg's job to keep the ponies under control. If she can't do that, I'm afraid she must go."

Ellie stood defiantly on the damaged lawn

as she watched her parents walk indoors. Meg had allowed her more freedom with her ponies than she had ever had before. Ellie didn't want to lose her, and she didn't want a new groom who might take that freedom away.

Somehow she had to find out who was making the mysterious hoofprints.

Chapter 2

By dinnertime that evening, Ellie had decided that there was only one way she could solve the mystery. She would have to watch all night to see what happened in the royal garden. If more hoofprints appeared, she would know exactly where they had come from. Her parents would have to believe her then.

Halfway through her lemon meringue

pie, she had an awful thought. Suppose her parents still didn't believe her? Suppose they thought she was making the story up to save Meg? For a moment, she felt too miserable to continue eating. Then she realized that there was a way to prove she was telling the truth. She would have to *catch* the pony that was wrecking the garden!

As soon as she had finished eating, Ellie went to the stable to collect everything she needed. She didn't want to worry Meg by telling her the plan, so she pretended she had come to help check on the ponies. Moonbeam, the palomino, saw her arrive and whinnied a welcome. Rainbow immediately popped her gray head over the door of her stall to see what was happening. Ellie stroked each of them and made a big show of checking that their doors were securely fastened.

Meg came over, clutching a handful of brass clips. "We'll put these on all the doors tonight, not just Sundance's. He might have been teaching the others his trick."

Ellie took one and walked over to the last stall. Shadow, the black Shetland, was busy eating hay, but when she called his name he walked over to get some peppermints.

Ellie gave him one, and he crunched it happily as she put the clip on the bolt.

She waited beside him until Meg got busy in Gypsy's stall. Then she slipped into the feed room and stuffed her pockets with carrots.

Her next stop was the tack room. She quickly grabbed a spare halter and stashed it under her fleece. Then she crossed her arms in front of her to hide the bulge and went back to the stable entrance.

Meg shut Gypsy's door, slid the bolt into position, and fastened it there with the clip. "They're all shut in firmly, so they can't possibly get out." She paused for a moment with a worried expression on her face and added, "But that's what I thought last night. I wish I knew what was going on."

"So do I," said Ellie, as Gypsy reached out toward her with his elegant nose. The gray thoroughbred had smelled the carrots and was determined to grab one.

Without thinking, Ellie unfolded her arms to push him away gently. But she quickly folded them again when she felt the halter start to slide out from under her fleece. She didn't want any awkward questions.

Gypsy was undeterred. He sniffed Ellie's pocket and pulled gently at the edge of it with his teeth. Ellie edged backward out of reach and called to Meg, "Bye. I'm heading back now."

"See you tomorrow," Meg called back. "Let's hope there are no hoofprints in the morning."

Ellie smiled as she ran back to the palace. If there were more hoofprints, she would know who was making them.

It was hard to stay calm for the rest of the evening. But Ellie was determined not to arouse suspicion by doing anything unusual.

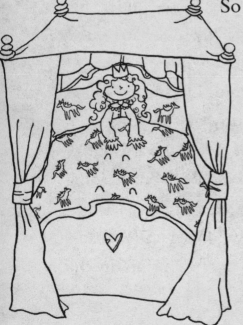

So she watched TV in her very pink bedroom for an hour or so. Then she ordered hot chocolate and cake and was already in her pink four-poster bed when the maid brought it in on a silver tray.

At the moment

when Ellie finished eating, the Queen came in to kiss her good night. Ellie lay down obediently, snuggled against into the pink satin pillow, and pretended to be going to sleep. But as soon as her mother had gone, she leaped out of bed and got dressed. No one else was likely to come to her room now, and the deep, soft mattress was much too comfortable. She couldn't risk falling asleep.

Suddenly, she heard footsteps coming up the spiral staircase. She dived back under the covers just in time, pulling them up to her chin to hide the fact that she was fully dressed. There was a gentle tap on the door. Then it swung open, and Miss Stringle came in. "I've just come to say good night," she said.

Ellie looked at her in surprise. Her

governess hardly ever did that.

"Your parents said you were very quiet at dinner. I thought I should check to see if you're feeling okay."

"I'm fine," said Ellie, as brightly as she could. She nodded toward her empty plate. "I've even had some late dessert."

"Are you absolutely sure?" asked Miss Stringle. She pulled a bottle of dark liquid from her pocket and added, "I brought some tonic just in case."

Ellie gulped. Miss Stringle's tonic was a gruesome mixture of cod-liver oil and molasses. It tasted foul. "I'm sure I don't need that," she said. "I'm perfectly all right."

"Sleep well, then," said Miss Stringle, as she reluctantly put the bottle back in her pocket. "And don't forget to brush your teeth." She started to leave. Then she stopped and glanced around the room.

Ellie held her breath as her governess looked straight at the pile of carrots in the middle of the rose pink carpet. If only she hadn't left them there. If only she had taken the time to hide them.

Luckily, Miss Stringle's eyes immediately moved on, taking in the dirty clothes, discarded tiaras, and half-read books, which lay everywhere in a big mess.

"Your room is a disgrace, Your Highness," she said, as she wrinkled her nose in disgust. "You must tell your maid to tidy it up."

"I will," Ellie promised, anxious to get

Miss Stringle out of the room as quickly as possible. She pretended to yawn. "Can I go to sleep now? I'm so tired."

To her relief, Miss Stringle agreed, and strode out of the room. As soon as her footsteps had faded into the distance, Ellie jumped out of bed again. She opened the door slightly and crouched beside it, waiting for everyone else to go to sleep.

Gradually, the sounds of the palace quieted. When everything was silent, she stuffed the carrots into the pockets of her pink jeans, and pulled on a thick jacket and Wellington boots. Then she grabbed the halter and a flashlight and crept out of the room.

The palace was eerily silent in the dim glow of the security lights. Ellie walked as quietly as she could down the spiral staircase to the main corridor. She peered both ways to make sure no one was around. Then she turned left and headed toward the back door, keeping close to the wall, in case she might suddenly need to jump into a doorway to hide.

Her heart was pounding as she listened for the faintest sound of anyone coming down the hallway.

The portraits on the wall stared down at her, making her feel as though she were being watched. This was already more frightening than she'd expected, and she wasn't even outside yet.

She was tempted to turn and run—to go back to bed and forget the whole plan. But she couldn't. She was determined to find out who was making the mysterious hoofprints in the royal garden.

If she didn't, Meg might end up losing her job.

Chapter 3

Ellie was relieved when she reached the back door without being discovered. She slid back the bolts, turned the handle, and stepped out into the starry night.

As soon as she closed the door behind her, she felt completely alone in the darkness.

She shivered with fear, wishing Kate were with her. It wouldn't have been as frightening if she had had a friend to share her midnight adventure with.

Ellie clicked on her flashlight and immediately felt better when she saw the beam of light shine on the ground ahead. The crescent moon was bright enough only to help her make out large shapes and the outlines of trees against the sky. It wouldn't stop her from tripping over something small and making a sound.

Ellie headed for the royal garden, walking slowly so as to make as little noise as possible on the gravel path. As soon as she could, she stepped onto the lawn. Walking on grass was much quieter.

Suddenly, her heart skipped a beat as a mysterious shape swooped toward her.

She saw a strange gleam of white—then the "ghost" flapped its wings and flew on.

Ellie breathed a sigh of relief. It wasn't anything spooky. It was just a barn owl. She swung her flashlight around, looking for a place to hide—somewhere she could keep watch secretly without being seen. Close beside the palace wall she found the storage box that held the croquet mallets and the cushions for the garden thrones. It was the perfect spot.

As she approached it, a pair of eyes glittered in the beam of the flashlight. They seemed to move straight toward her, unblinking and menacing. Ellie froze, remembering tales of wolves attacking travelers at night. Then she felt something soft rub against her legs.

Ellie's fear dissolved as she realized whom the eyes belonged to. She reached down and picked up Tibbs. It was good to have some company. If Kate couldn't be there, her cat would have to do instead.

Ellie wriggled in behind the storage box and found a place where she could sit facing the lawn. From there, she was sure she would be able to see any ponies that came visiting in the moonlight. She made herself as comfortable as possible and settled down to watch.

Tibbs curled up on her lap and started to purr. Ellie relaxed as she stroked his soft fur. For the first time that night, she started to enjoy being out under the starry sky.

Time ticked by, but nothing happened. Even the owl kept still and quiet. Gradually,

Ellie became more and more aware of how cold and hard the ground was. She fidgeted and moved from side to side, trying to make herself more comfortable. The movement disturbed Tibbs, who stopped purring and stared at her in disgust. Then he wandered off in a huff and disappeared into the darkness.

Ellie felt lonely without him. She also felt very tired. She yawned again and wondered what Kate was doing. Was it nighttime in the desert? Were there any horses to ride, or just camels? Then Ellie's eyelids drooped and she fell asleep.

It was the cold that woke her. It had seeped through her clothes and boots, chilling her bones and freezing her toes. She grumbled

to herself as she pulled her jacket tighter and shivered. How could she have been so stupid? How long had she been asleep?

She peered out at the lawn and saw to her dismay that dawn was already breaking. She had been asleep for hours.

If more hoofprints had appeared while she was sleeping, her plan would have failed.

Suddenly, she heard a loud rustling noise.

She leaped to her feet and crouched behind the storage box, ready to run at a moment's notice. The noise came again. It was closer this time. Something big was coming toward the garden.

Chapter 4

Ellie held her breath as she waited for the creature to appear. Then, finally, she saw the answer to the mystery. Silhouetted against the dawn sky was a pony. But it wasn't Moonbeam, Sundance, Shadow, Rainbow, or Gypsy. This was a strange pony—one she had never seen before.

The animal walked onto the lawn and started to graze. It was a bay mare who looked as though she had been living wild for ages. Her reddish brown coat was dirty, and her long black mane and tail were matted and tangled. But despite the obvious neglect, she was sturdy. The long, shaggy hair that hung down over her hooves made her look like a miniature cart horse.

Ellie smiled with satisfaction as she watched the pony eat the few remaining flowers. Her plan had worked. She had solved the mystery. Now, she just had to

catch the mysterious visitor, so she could prove the pony's existence to everyone else.

She reached down and picked up the halter. Then she tucked it behind her back and started to walk across the lawn. The pony lifted her head from the flowers and watched Ellie warily.

"Good girl," called Ellie quietly, in what she hoped was a soothing voice. "Stay there. No one's going to hurt you." She circled around to the other side of the pony.

Gradually, she got closer and closer, keeping her body turned slightly to the side so she wasn't directly facing the pony. It was a trick she had read somewhere in one of her pony books, and this seemed the right moment to try it out.

At first, it seemed to work. The bay mare

stood still until Ellie was only a couple of feet away. Then the pony started to edge backward. She looked frightened and ready to run. Ellie decided she couldn't risk waiting. She lunged forward and grabbed for the pony's mane.

The mare saw her coming. With a loud squeal, she swung around and raced off, sending chunks of lawn flying from underneath her galloping hooves. Ellie had missed her completely, and she crashed to the ground, squashing the last of her mother's favorite petunias.

She struggled to her feet just in time to see the strange pony jump a low hedge and vanish around the side of the palace. Ellie raced after her, still clutching the halter. But she couldn't run as fast as the pony. When she rounded the corner of the palace, there was no sign of the animal at all.

For a moment, Ellie thought she had lost her. Then she spotted a trail of flattened flowers and damaged bushes and set off in pursuit again. To her delight, the trail led to the only entrance to the kitchen garden.

I've caught you now, she thought as she slipped quietly inside and closed the gate behind her. The garden was surrounded by a high brick wall. There was no way the pony could escape this time.

The bay mare was standing in the middle

of the neat rows of vegetables, munching on a head of lettuce. When she saw Ellie arrive, she lifted her head and stared at her suspiciously. A green leaf fell out of the side of her mouth.

Ellie took a couple of steps toward her. The pony took a couple of steps back. Ellie moved forward again. The pony tossed her head and trotted off to another part of the garden. This time Ellie stayed still. There was no point in trying to move any closer. The pony wasn't going to allow that.

After a few moments, the bay mare lost interest in Ellie and started exploring the garden again. She wandered along a row of tomatoes, pulling up the plants one by one and tossing them over her shoulder. Then she turned her attention to the cabbages.

Oh, no! thought Ellie. The gardeners would be horrified when they saw what had happened to their hard work. Somehow, she had to catch the pony, but the poor creature was too frightened. She must have been living wild for a long time. How could Ellie win her confidence?

Ellie leaned against the wall and wondered what to do. The dawn air was chilly. She pushed her hands into her pockets to warm them up, and felt the carrots.

She'd forgotten all about those. Perhaps they would help. She pulled one out and put it into the palm of her outstretched hand. Then she held it in front of her and called, "Here, girl. Look what I've got."

The pony turned and looked at her. Ellie waved the carrot gently and took a step toward her. This time, the pony didn't move away. Instead, she pointed her nose at Ellie and sniffed the air.

Ellie tossed the carrot forward so that it landed a foot or so in front of the bay mare. The pony sniffed again. Then, slowly and cautiously, she edged forward and grabbed it with her teeth. As she crunched, she watched Ellie carefully.

"Do you want some more?" asked Ellie. She threw another carrot, but not as far as she had thrown the previous one. The pony walked forward again and ate it.

Great! She's a carrot addict, thought Ellie. She threw another one, and then another. The pony came a little closer each time, and each time she seemed a little more confident.

Soon, the pony was only a couple of feet away. Ellie was tempted to try to grab her, but she knew that that might be a disaster. If she frightened the pony now, she might not be able to win her trust later.

Ellie pulled another carrot from her pocket. But this time she didn't throw it. Instead, she held it out and walked very slowly toward the bay mare.

The pony arched her neck and snorted. But she didn't move. Her eyes were fixed on the carrot. She moved her nose forward cautiously, her nostrils twitching with delight at the smell. Then she gently took the carrot from Ellie's hand and started eating.

Ellie stood still and delighted in the feel of the pony's soft velvety lips. She reached out slowly and stroked the pony's dusty face. The animal flinched slightly. Then she relaxed and nuzzled Ellie's pocket in search of another carrot.

Very gently, Ellie slipped the halter over the pony's nose. As she fastened it behind her ears, she felt a surge of triumph. Everyone would have to believe her now.

Chapter 5

Ellie was dying to show the new pony to her parents. But they were still in bed, and she knew they wouldn't appreciate being woken up. So she took the bay mare back to the yard and tied her up, then shook out clean straw to make a bed in a spare stall. When she had finished, she filled a hay net and put a bucket of clean water in the corner.

"I'd better give you a name," she said, as

she led the bay mare into the stable. She stroked the pony's head and spotted a faded white mark in the middle of her forehead. Her coat was so dirty that Ellie hadn't noticed it before. "You have a star between your eyes, and there were many stars in the sky last night. I think I'll call you Starlight."

The pony seemed to approve. She whinnied softly and rubbed her head against Ellie's shoulder. Ellie slipped off the halter and went outside. Although she was tired after her night in the open air, she was much too excited to go back to bed. So she stayed in the field, eager to show off her great discovery.

Meg soon arrived. "What are you doing here so early in the morning?" she asked. Then she spotted Starlight. "And where on earth did that pony come from?"

"She's the mystery pony who's been making all the hoofprints," replied Ellie. She quickly explained what had happened, ending triumphantly with, "I caught her all by myself."

"Well done," said Meg. "Although I'm not sure that staying out all night was a good idea."

"I was perfectly safe," said Ellie. "There are guards all around the palace grounds."

The King and Queen came to the stable as soon as they heard the news. They were followed by a maid carrying their early-morning tea on a silver tray.

Ellie told them the whole story while they drank their tea. "See? I was telling the truth. And so was Meg."

"I suppose you were, my dear," said the King, in an offhand way that didn't quite count as an apology. He drained the last drops of tea from his gold-rimmed cup and handed it back to the maid.

The Queen reached out to stroke Starlight, but changed her mind when she saw how dirty she was. "It's hard to believe that there was a pony living wild on the palace grounds and nobody knew anything about it."

"Quite amazing," agreed the King. "But I do wish you wouldn't take things into your own hands, Aurelia. One day, one of your crazy plans will get you into trouble."

"But I wouldn't have had to think of this one if you'd believed me in the first place," said Ellie, trying to lay the blame firmly at her parents' doorstep.

The King ignored her completely and turned his attention to Starlight. "Now we just have to decide what to do with the pony."

Ellie stared at him in surprise. "She'll stay here, of course. She's mine. I found her."

The Queen shook her head. "Life's not like that, my dear. All ponies belong to someone, even wild ones. We'll have to find Starlight's owner and give her back."

"But that's not fair," said Ellie.

"Yes, it is," said the Queen, with a firmness that suggested that her mind was already made up.

The King peered over the stall door and looked disapprovingly at Starlight. "She's not the right kind of pony for a princess, anyway. She's much too big and heavy." He paused thoughtfully and added, "We'll tell the papers about her. They always love a royal story."

The Queen looked at Ellie with a concerned expression. "Maybe we should wait until tomorrow. That would give Aurelia time to catch up on her sleep."

The King shook his head. "It would also give her time to get attached to the pony," he explained. "The sooner this is done, the better."

"I suppose you're right, my dear," replied

the Queen. Then she turned to Ellie and said, "The reporters are sure to want to talk to you, Aurelia. I'll ask Miss Stringle to give you a quick lesson on how a true princess should handle questions from the press."

"But it's my vacation," protested Ellie.

"That's got nothing to do with it," said the King. "You have to be prepared to meet the press today. We need this story on the front page to make sure that the pony's owners read it."

Ellie desperately hoped that they wouldn't. She had already fallen in love with Starlight and didn't want to lose her.

Chapter 6

Ellie went unwillingly to the schoolroom after breakfast. Miss Stringle was waiting for her. She seemed much more enthusiastic about the extra lesson than her student was.

Miss Stringle made Ellie stand up straight beside her desk, while she sat down opposite on a hard wooden chair. "Now, pretend I'm the press and tell me the story of how you found the pony. Remember, you've got to capture my interest. So, make it exciting! Make it dramatic!"

Ellie did the best she could, but Miss Stringle soon interrupted. "No, no, no! You mustn't tell them that you stayed out all night. You're a princess. We can't have the whole world knowing you misbehaved."

"But what if they ask why I was out there?" asked Ellie.

"Just smile and say, 'I'm very glad you asked me that.' Then ignore the question and go on talking about something completely different."

Ellie stared at her doubtfully. "Are you sure that will work?"

"It always does for the prime minister," replied Miss Stringle. "Now let me hear the whole story again, but this time minus the part about staying out all night."

Ellie told the story over and over, until her governess was finally satisfied that it was perfect. Then she had to practice smiling for the photographers—or, more precisely, for Miss Stringle, who rushed around pretending that her handbag was a camera.

At long last, her governess agreed the lesson was over. Ellie breathed a sigh of relief and ran off to the stables. She found Meg sweeping the yard and asked, "Can I groom Starlight?"

Meg laughed. "It'll take more than a brush to get her clean. I think we'd better give her a bath."

Ellie was surprised. She'd never washed a pony before. She got Starlight from her stall and tied her up in a sunny part of the yard.

The bay mare was pleased to see her and nuzzled her pockets for carrots.

Meg handed Ellie a bucket of water. "Start with her tail and leave her head for last. That's the part she might really dislike."

Ellie swished the end of Starlight's tail in the bucket. The water immediately changed color. "There's loads of dirt coming out," she said.

"Good," said Meg, pouring a jug of water on the rest of the tail.

Ellie put the bucket down, squirted some horse shampoo into her hands, and rubbed it into the pony's wet hair. Soon, Starlight's tail was covered with lather, and so was Ellie's shirt.

"Should we rinse her now?" asked Ellie.

"Not until we've washed her all over," said Meg. She started pouring water over Starlight's back and legs.

Ellie followed behind, rubbing in the shampoo. She was surprised to find that the pony's ribs were only just under her skin. Although she was heavily built, she certainly wasn't fat. In fact, she was thinner than any of Ellie's other ponies.

Starlight stood perfectly still as they

covered her body and mane with soap bubbles. But she flinched when Meg tried to wash her face.

Meg stepped to one side and handed the jug to Ellie.

"You'd better do this," she said. "You're the one she trusts."

Very gently, Ellie dampened Starlight's face and rubbed in the shampoo. She was careful to avoid the pony's eyes. She knew how much shampoo could sting. Then, equally gently, she rinsed away the bubbles. She could see the improvement immediately. The dirty gray mark between the pony's eyes was now a pure white star.

"That's terrific," said Meg. "Now use the hose to rinse the rest of her." She turned on the tap so that the water dribbled out slowly.

Ellie had to stand close to Starlight to rinse her. The water trickled down her arms and splashed onto her legs. Soon she was almost as wet as the pony, but she didn't mind. It felt good to see the streams of water carrying away the dirt.

Eventually, all the bubbles had gone, and the pony was clean.

"She can dry off in the sun," said Meg, as she tied up a hay net for Starlight to eat from. Then she went into the tack room and returned carrying two mugs of steaming hot chocolate.

Ellie drank hers while sitting in the sunshine beside Starlight. When they were both warm and dry, she carefully brushed the tangles out of the pony's mane and tail. Then she took a few steps back and smiled as she admired her efforts.

Starlight looked very different now. Her brown coat gleamed, and her black tail hung smooth and straight. It nearly reached the ground. Her black mane was long, too. It cascaded over her deep, strong neck until it was level with her shoulders.

"You've done a good job," said Meg. "Once she's put on a bit of weight, she'll look fantastic."

Ellie glowed with pride. "Should I get the scissors and cut those long hairs on her feet?" she asked.

"Absolutely not," said Meg. "They're called feathers, and they look perfect on a pony like her."

Suddenly, a voice called out, "Princess Aurelia." Ellie turned and saw her governess,

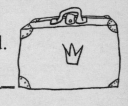

Miss Stringle, striding into the yard. She was wearing a sensible brown suit with sensible brown shoes and clutching a sensible brown suitcase.

"Are you going away?" asked Ellie, hopefully. There could be no more extra lessons if her governess weren't around to give them.

"Of course not," said Miss Stringle, who was staring disapprovingly at Ellie's dirty clothes. "The press will be here any minute, and we can't have your picture in the papers looking like that."

Ellie groaned. She didn't want to talk to the reporters. She didn't want her photograph taken. But most of all, she didn't want to help find Starlight's owner.

Chapter 7

Ellie followed Miss Stringle unwillingly into the tack room. It felt all wrong having her governess there. This was supposed to be the place where she could escape from lessons and palace rules.

The only table in the room was piled high with saddle soap, spare stirrups, and saddle-cloths. Miss Stringle sighed as she pushed the mess to one side to make room for the suitcase. Then she snapped the suitcase open and pulled out some clothes. "Quickly: put these on," she ordered.

Ellie cringed. The frilly pink dress and silver sandals would look ridiculous in the stable. "I can't wear those here," she argued.

"Oh, yes, you can," said Miss Stringle firmly. "The public have expectations of princesses. It's your duty to look the part."

Hmmm, thought Ellie, as she reluctantly got changed.

When Ellie was ready, Miss Stringle checked her from head to toe and carefully balanced a glittering tiara on Ellie's unruly curls. Then she spat neatly into a white lace-trimmed, handkerchief and wiped Ellie's nose.

"That will have to do," she said, without enthusiasm. "You'd better go and meet the reporters. And for heaven's sake, try to remember everything I've told you."

Ellie walked nervously toward the tack-room door. She had never done anything like this on her own before, and she had a feeling it might be harder than her rehearsal with Miss Stringle had been. Her lack of confidence wasn't helped by her uncomfortable royal outfit. She would have felt much happier in her jodhpurs.

As soon as Ellie stepped outside, she was surrounded by a crowd of reporters. Cameras snapped, and microphones were pushed in front of her face. She looked around in desperation, longing to get back

the peace of the tack room. But her escape route had already been blocked.

"Give the princess some space," commanded Miss Stringle.

For the first time in her life, Ellie was pleased that her governess was so bossy. To her relief, the reporters and cameramen stepped back. They looked like naughty schoolchildren who had just been scolded by their teacher.

From then on, Miss Stringle took full

command of the press conference. She insisted that the reporters stand in neat rows, and she made them raise their hands before asking their questions.

Ellie introduced them to Starlight and told them how she had used carrots to catch the pony in the kitchen garden. She made sure they realized that she had done it all by herself, but she remembered not to mention creeping out at night without permission.

At first, Starlight stood patiently while she had her photograph taken over and over again. But she soon became bored with all the attention. She nuzzled Ellie's pink dress in search of carrots. Then she rubbed her head against Ellie's right shoulder, knocking her slightly off balance. Ellie stumbled, and her tiara slipped down over her left ear.

Before she had time to straighten it, Starlight lifted her nose and blew gently, straight into Ellie's face. As Ellie's eyes widened in surprise, she again heard the cameras clicking away. With a horrible certainty, she guessed which of the many pictures would be on the front page.

She was right. The next morning, every paper in the land carried a photo of a wide-cycd Ellie with her tiara over one ear and Starlight's nose in front of the other.

Miss Stringle was appalled, but the King wasn't. "It's wonderful publicity," he explained after breakfast. "Everyone's going to look at that picture. It should guarantee that Starlight's owner sees it."

Ellie stared at the papers laid out on the huge mahogany table. "Maybe they won't see it," she suggested hopefully. "Maybe everyone will be so busy laughing at me that they won't read about Starlight."

The Queen smiled. "I don't think so, Aurelia. No one can ignore those headlines."

Just then, a maid came in and whispered something to the King. He listened to her carefully. Then he leaned back in his chair and smiled with satisfaction. "I knew my plan would work," he said. "A man who thinks Starlight is his lost pony has arrived. He's on his way to the stable now."

Ellie leaped to her feet in alarm and raced out of the room. She was desperate to reach the stable before the man did. Losing Starlight would be awful. It would be even worse if he took her away before Ellie had a chance to say good-bye.

Chapter 8

Ellie raced into the yard so fast that she nearly collided with the visitor.

"This is Tidy Jack," said Meg.

His name didn't suit him at all. His jacket and jeans were filthy. His boots were caked with mud, and his hair looked as if it hadn't been combed for a week. "You must be the little lady who found my pony," he said, thrusting out a dirty hand.

Ellie didn't shake it. Instead, she pulled herself up to her full height and said, firmly, "I am not a little lady. I am a princess."

"Of course you are, my dear," said Tidy Jack, with a smile that revealed tobacco-stained teeth. "Please pardon my mistake." But only his lips were smiling. His blue eyes were cold and mocking.

Ellie didn't like him at all. She didn't want to be near him. So she walked on ahead and arrived at Starlight's stall first. The bay mare was standing quietly eating hay. She whinnied softly when she saw Ellie.

Then Starlight saw Tidy Jack, and her behavior changed

instantly. She moved as close to the opposite wall as she could, flattening her ears against her neck in alarm.

"That looks like my Flo," the man said. He reached out to touch her, but pulled his hand back quickly when Starlight lunged at him. Her teeth snapped shut on empty air where his fingers had been only a second before. "That's her, all right," he said. "She always did have a nasty temper."

"No, she doesn't," said Ellie. "She's really gentle with me."

But Ellie was wasting her breath. Tidy Jack wasn't listening. He was busy arranging to take Starlight away. "I'll be back in a couple of hours with a trailer," he told Meg, before marching out of the yard.

As soon as he'd gone, Ellie burst into

tears. "I don't like him, and neither does Starlight. I don't want her to go to someone so mean."

Meg put her arm round Ellie's shoulders and hugged her. "I feel the same way. But there's nothing we can do about it—he's her owner."

Ellie refused to give up. "I'll ask my dad," she announced. "He's the King. He can do anything."

She ran back to the palace and found him reading important papers in his office. To her disappointment, he was as negative as Meg. "There's nothing I can do," he said. "I know I have power, but I have to be fair. And it wouldn't be fair to take Starlight away from her owner."

"But she doesn't like him," said Ellie.

67

The King sighed. "You're probably imagining it. I'm sure everything will work out for the best in the end." He turned back to his papers. As far as he was concerned, the conversation was over.

Ellie knew there was no point in arguing anymore, but she wasn't ready to give up. She walked slowly back to the stable, wondering what else she could do. Before she could think of a plan, she spotted Meg riding Starlight around the field.

"I thought we'd make the most of her while she's still here," Meg called as she brought the pony to a stop and dismounted. "She's a lovely ride. Do you want to try?"

"Of course I do," said Ellie, her eyes bright with excitement. She got her pink-and-gold hard hat from the tack room and mounted as quickly as she could. It felt strange to be on a different pony. She had never ridden one with such a broad back before.

Meg rode alongside Ellie on Gypsy. They spent a while walking and trotting until Ellie felt a little more confident. Then Meg suggested a canter. "You'll have to be firm," she said. "She'll do as she's told, but only if you tell her properly. Give it a try."

Ellie bit her lip nervously. She knew that cantering in the field was one of her weak points. There were so many things to remember that she always seemed to forget one of them. As they trotted up to the next corner, she shortened the reins and pushed hard on Starlight's sides with her legs. The bay mare speeded up, but she didn't canter. Instead, she broke into a very fast, bouncy trot.

Meg laughed. "You forgot to sit down in the saddle," she said.

Ellie steadied the pony at a more comfortable speed. Then, at the next corner, she tried going faster again. This time, she did everything right and, to her delight, Starlight broke into a slow canter. It was very comfortable—just like riding a rocking horse.

The bay mare was obviously enjoying herself. She went faster and faster, speeding up a little more each time they went around a corner.

"Steady," said Meg. "You mustn't let her run away with you."

Ellie smiled with satisfaction as she pulled back on the reins and slowed the pony to a trot. Meg's words had given her an idea—an idea that just might save Starlight from Tidy Jack.

Chapter 9

The idea buzzed around Ellie's head as she rode back to the yard. Suppose Starlight were to run away. Suppose Tidy Jack found only an empty stall when he came back with his trailer. It would be impossible for him to take her then.

"Can you unsaddle her by yourself?" asked Meg. "I have to go down to the village for some stamps, but I'll be back long before that man turns up to get her."

Ellie agreed with enthusiasm. Perhaps this was a sign that she was doing the right thing. It would give her a chance to put her idea into action without Meg seeing.

She quickly took off Starlight's saddle and bridle, and put on a halter instead. Then she led the bay mare out of the yard and along the path toward the deer park. She tried to look confident, but she wasn't. Her stomach was churning with nerves. At any moment she expected someone to stop her and ask what she was doing.

"I'll just say I'm taking you out to graze for a while," she told Starlight. "No one can argue about that."

She led the pony through the gate at the end of the path and closed it carefully behind her. Tears misted her eyes as she gave Starlight one last hug. Then she unbuckled the halter and slipped it off. "It's time to say good-bye," she whispered sadly.

Ellie waited for Starlight to gallop off into the distance. But the pony didn't go anywhere. She just stood still and stared at Ellie.

Ellie waved her hands at her. "Off you go," she said. "You're free now."

Starlight shook her head, sending her long black mane cascading in all directions. But she stayed exactly where she was.

Ellie gave her a push.

Starlight still didn't budge.

"Maybe she's waiting for me to go," thought Ellie. She walked toward the gate. Starlight followed.

"No, no, no," said Ellie in despair. It was

impossible to open the gate without the pony barging through. So she climbed over it instead and started to walk back toward the stable. Perhaps Starlight would go once she realized Ellie wasn't staying.

But Starlight didn't go. Instead, she hung her head over the gate and whinnied pitifully. She obviously didn't want to be left behind.

Ellie felt very mean. She nearly ran back to get Starlight. But she knew if she did that she'd have to give the pony to Tidy Jack. Surely it was kinder to abandon her than to hand her over to someone she was so afraid of.

She forced herself to keep walking away. To her relief, the whinnying stopped. She looked back and saw Starlight trotting away from the gate. At last, her plan was working.

Then Starlight stopped and turned around. She galloped toward the gate at full speed. Ellie watched in horror. She was sure the pony was going to crash into the gate and hurt herself!

But she didn't. Instead, she jumped the gate perfectly, soaring over it to land safely on the other side. Then she whinnied again and cantered happily up to Ellie. There was no way she was going to be left behind.

Ellie was delighted to know that Starlight loved her so much, but she was really upset that her plan had failed. Then she had another idea. "If I can't make you run away, I'll just have to pretend that you have," she explained, as she put the pony's halter on again, hoping her new plan would work.

She led the bay mare into the barn and tied her up in the corner farthest from the door. Then she moved some bales of straw to form a barrier stopping anyone from seeing the pony from the barn door. It wasn't perfect, but it was the best she could do in the time available.

When Ellie got back to the yard, Meg was standing in front of the empty stable. "Where's Starlight?" she asked.

"She ran away," Ellie replied, trying hard to look upset. This was the first test of her story. She had to make it work.

Meg looked surprised. "How did she get out?"

Ellie hesitated. It was such an obvious question. If only she had thought of an answer in advance. Then she remembered Miss Stringle's advice. "I'm very glad you asked me that," she said, with a smile. "Aren't we having nice weather for this time of year?"

Meg burst out laughing. "I don't know what you're up to, Ellie, but imitating the prime minister isn't going to help."

Their conversation was interrupted by the arrival of the King and Queen. Ellie was surprised to see them. She was even more surprised to see that they were not alone. Walking between them was a plump lady with gray hair who looked overwhelmed by all the royal attention.

"This is Mrs. Grant," said the King. "She thinks Starlight belongs to her."

Chapter 10

Ellie felt confused. "How can two people own the same pony?" she asked.

"They can't," said the King. "That's why your mother and I are here. We want to find out what's going on."

"Star vanished from her field more than a year ago," the plump lady explained sadly. "I've been so worried about her. It would be wonderful if you've found her." She smiled.

It was a real smile, not at all like Tidy Jack's. It lit up her face and made her brown eyes sparkle.

Ellie smiled back. She liked this woman as much as she disliked Tidy Jack. She could see how much she loved and missed her pony. It would not be so bad giving Starlight back to her.

"Come and meet our mystery pony," said the King, leading Mrs. Grant toward Starlight's stall. "Then we'll know for sure if she's yours or not."

Meg stepped in front of them. "I'm afraid she's not there at the moment."

"Where is she?" asked the Queen.

Meg gave Ellie a gentle push in their direction. "I think the princess is the best person to answer that," she said.

Ellie didn't know what to do. It was impossible to tell whether Mrs. Grant really owned Starlight without letting her see the pony. But doing that meant abandoning her plan to pretend the bay mare had run away. If it turned out that Starlight really belonged to Tidy Jack, she would have no way to stop him from taking the pony away.

"Come on, Aurelia, don't play games," said the Queen, impatiently. "We haven't got all day."

"I do hope nothing's happened to her," asked Mrs. Grant.

The kindness and concern in the lady's voice helped Ellie to make up her mind. She decided she had to tell the truth and just hope everything would work out all right in the end. "Starlight's in the barn," she admitted. Then she realized she should probably give some sort of explanation, so she added, "I thought the change of scene would do her good."

Meg raised her eyebrows. Then a slow smile spread over her face, as if she'd guessed Ellie's plan. "Well, as they say, a change is as good as a vacation," she said, with a wink in Ellie's direction. "Now, Ellie, show us where she is."

Ellie led them to the barn and showed them where Starlight was hidden, behind the bales of straw.

"It *is* Star!" exclaimed Mrs. Grant. She

rushed up to the bay mare and threw her arms around the pony's neck.

Starlight didn't flinch as she had when Tidy Jack tried to touch her. Instead, she whinnied a welcome and rubbed her head against the woman's chest. Mrs. Grant laughed and pulled a carrot from her pocket. "I hope you still like these," she said. She held it out to the pony, who crunched it happily.

"There's no doubt she belongs to you," said Ellie.

"None at all," said Meg.

"Which leaves us with the mystery of Tidy Jack," said the King, as he led the way out of the barn. Mrs. Grant and Ellie walked on either side of Starlight, but Ellie kept hold of the pony's rope.

They had just arrived in the yard when Tidy Jack strolled in, whistling confidently. He was swinging a filthy halter in time with the tune when he spotted Mrs. Grant. The whistle died on his lips as he stared at her in dismay.

"That man!" shouted Mrs. Grant. "I saw him hanging around Star's field the day she disappeared."

Tidy Jack turned and fled, dropping the halter as he ran.

"Stop, thief!" yelled the King.

A couple of palace guards raced up in response. Tidy Jack was in such a panic that he didn't see them in time. He bumped into them at top speed, fell over, and landed in a prickly holly bush.

He looked miserable as the guards pulled him out and arrested him for stealing Starlight.

"I don't think he'll be bothering you again," said the Queen to Mrs. Grant.

Ellie pushed Starlight's rope into the plump lady's hands. "You can take her now," she said, blinking hard to drive away the tears that filled her eyes.

Mrs. Grant looked at Starlight and then at Ellie. "I don't know," she said. "My arthritis acts up when I'm mucking out on cold mornings. And there's no one to ride Star, now that my son's moved to the city. Would you like to keep her?"

Ellie could hardly believe her ears. "Of course I would!" She tried to look calm and dignified, but inside she was bouncing up and down with excitement.

"Wait a minute," said the King. "I think I have some say in this."

Mrs. Grant put her hand up to her face in dismay. "I'm dreadfully sorry, Your Majesty. I should have asked your permission first. But it would be so good for the pony and good for me."

"I know," sighed the King. "But I'm afraid Starlight is not really the right sort of pony for a princess. She's a bit on the heavy side."

Ellie opened her mouth to argue, but her

mother spoke before she had even started.

"And what's wrong with that?" asked the Queen, patting her own rather ample hips. "People don't have to be slim to be beautiful, and neither do ponies."

The King looked embarrassed. "I suppose you're right, my dear," he muttered sheepishly.

The Queen smiled. "That's settled, then. Starlight stays."

Mrs. Grant pushed the halter rope back into Ellie's hands. "She's all yours," she announced.

Ellie forgot all about acting like a princess and gave Mrs. Grant a huge

hug as she showered her with thanks.

Then she hugged Starlight and whispered, "I'm glad you didn't run away. We're going to be so happy together."

Here's a sneak peek at the next adventure
of the

Pony-Crazed Princess

in

Princess Ellie's Camping Trip

Princess Ellie's Camping Trip

Chapter 1

"They said yes!" yelled Princess Ellie as she ran into the yard. Her frilly pink dress looked ridiculous with her Wellington boots. But she didn't care. She was in too much of a hurry to share her good news.

"That's terrific," said her best friend, Kate. She bounced up and down with excitement, sending the water slopping over the edge of the bucket she was carrying.

Meg, the palace groom, put a bulging hay net beside Moonbeam's door. "I'm really happy for you. But I must admit I'm surprised. I didn't think the King and Queen would approve of you going camping."

"Neither did I," said Kate. She put the bucket beside the hay net and undid the bolt on the door. Moonbeam poked her head out to see what was happening. She spotted Ellie immediately and whinnied a welcome.

Ellie grinned and stroked the palomino's nose. "They didn't like the idea at first," she explained. "But the prime minister persuaded them it would do me some good. We'll be perfectly safe on the palace grounds, and he thinks it will be character-forming, whatever that means."

"I think it'll be fun," laughed Kate as she

swung Moonbeam's door open and carried the bucket inside.

"So do I," said Ellie. She picked up the hay net and followed her friend into the stall.

Moonbeam immediately started pulling out pieces of hay. She made the net bounce and jiggle so much that it was hard for Ellie to tie it to the ring on the wall.

Kate pushed the hungry pony away so that Ellie could finish quickly. Then she grabbed Ellie by the arm and pulled her impatiently toward the door. "Come on," she said. "I've got something really exciting to show you."

To find out what happens next, read

Princess Ellie's Camping Trip